This Little Tiger book belongs to:

_____

_____

_____

For Otis with love
~ M C B

For my sister-in-law Vicky Greensit
~ T M

LITTLE TIGER PRESS LTD,
an imprint of Little Tiger Group
1 The Coda Centre,
189 Munster Road, London SW6 6AW
www.littletiger.co.uk
First published in Great Britain 2016
This edition published 2017
Text copyright © M Christina Butler 2016
Illustrations copyright © Tina Macnaughton 2016

M Christina Butler and Tina Macnaughton have asserted
their rights to be identified as the author and illustrator of this
work under the Copyright, Designs and Patents Act, 1988

A CIP catalogue record for this book is available from the British Library
All rights reserved • ISBN 978-1-84869-272-5
Printed in China • LTP/1800/1821/0517
2 4 6 8 10 9 7 5 3 1

One Noisy Night

M Christina Butler • Tina Macnaughton

LITTLE TIGER

LONDON

It was very nearly Christmas. Little Hedgehog and his friends were having breakfast.

"Did you hear the creaking and crashing last night?" asked Rabbit.

"I certainly did," said Badger.

"I didn't hear a thing!" said Little Hedgehog. "Was it the snow melting?"

"It was louder than that," said Fox. "I'm going to find out what's going on!"

That night the noises
were louder than ever!

Creak!

Groan!

Crash!

Fox jumped up and crept outside.
As he tiptoed through the moonlit
trees, he saw a red hat bobbing
about near the river.
"Is that you, Little Hedgehog?" he cried.
But the hat disappeared, and
Fox went home even more
puzzled than before.

The next morning Fox went to see Little Hedgehog.

"What were you doing in the wood last night?" he asked.

"But I was at home!" replied Little Hedgehog.

"Oh," said Fox. "I was sure it was you! I must have been seeing things."

That night, the sounds
started again. Fox tiptoed
back into the wood and
bumped into Badger at the
riverbank.
"Do you know what's making
those noises?" asked Fox.
"No," whispered Badger. "But wait!
Is that Little Hedgehog?"
"It is!" cried Fox. "Quick! Follow me!"

But as Fox ran to the left, Badger turned
right and they bumped into each other
with a CRASH!

"You went the wrong way!"
cried Fox.
"I didn't," snapped Badger.
"Little Hedgehog was over there.
I'd know his red hat anywhere!"
"Humph. He's gone now,"
grumbled Fox. "We'll just have
to ask him tomorrow."

Next morning the friends rushed to Little Hedgehog's house.

"Hello!" he beamed. "I was just putting out these sandbags in case the river floods over Christmas."

"We saw you down there last night!" said Badger. "Whatever were you doing?"

"But I've not been near the river!" insisted Little Hedgehog.

"I'm *sure* it was him," mumbled Fox as they
walked home. "So why wouldn't he tell us?"
    "Perhaps he's planning a Christmas surprise,"
said Badger. "It's all very strange."

That evening, Little Hedgehog couldn't stop thinking about the strange noises. "I wonder what they are?" he thought. "They're nothing to do with me! I'll have to stay awake and find out for myself."

But it was so cosy by the fire, he soon fell fast asleep.

Suddenly a huge CRASH! shook the house.
"Oh my!" gasped Little Hedgehog.
And he rushed out into the moonlight.

Badger, Fox and Rabbit were already
by the river.

"Look over there!" cried Fox.
"It's Little Hedgehog!"

"No it isn't!" said an indignant
voice behind them. "I'm right here!"

Everyone spun round.
"If you're here," gulped
Rabbit, "who's that over there?"
"And there!" shouted Fox, pointing
to another red hat.
"Never mind that – look at the river!"
Little Hedgehog cried.
The water was swirling
higher and higher,
until . . .

. . . SWOOSH! The riverbank gave way and the water roared towards them.

"Get back!" yelled Little Hedgehog.

But Rabbit wasn't quick enough and he was swept off his feet!

"Quick!" squeaked
Little Hedgehog. "Hold on to me."
Rabbit clung tightly to Little Hedgehog
as Badger pulled them away from the swirling water.
"You saved Rabbit!" Badger cheered.

But now the water was sweeping over the bank and down through the wood!

"Help! Our homes will be washed away!" yelled Fox.

"Look!" Rabbit called out.

Two beavers in red woolly hats were pushing a huge tree towards them.

"They're trying to mend the bank and stop the flood!" cried Little Hedgehog. "Grab that tree – quick!"

Together they guided the tree towards the riverbank.

"Stand back!" called Little Hedgehog.

The tree groaned and stuck fast, and the water swirled back down the river again.

"It worked!" Fox cried.

"You've saved our homes from the flood," cheered Badger. "Well done, beavers! Let's all have some Christmas cocoa to celebrate!"

"So the red hats we saw were the beavers' not yours, Little Hedgehog!" grinned Badger.
"We were chopping down trees to make a dam in the river," they explained.
"And that's what the noises were!" laughed Fox.

"Thank you for rescuing me!" said Rabbit, smiling at Little Hedgehog.

"Hurrah for Little Hedgehog and the beavers!" cried Badger.

And the friends all cheered for the heroes in red hats!

More heart-warming stories from Little Tiger Press!

For information regarding any of the above titles or for our catalogue, please contact us:
Little Tiger Press, 1 The Coda Centre, 189 Munster Road, London SW6 6AW
Tel: 020 7385 6333 • E-mail: contact@littletiger.co.uk • www.littletiger.co.uk